# JACK RYDER

# STELLA
## FOR *Christmas*
### *Office Fantasy & Desires*
### Romance Erotica

# WARNING

This book contains sexually explicit scenes and adult language. It may be considered offensive to some readers. This book is for sale to adults ONLY.

* * * * * * * * * * * * * * * * * *

Please store your files wisely where they cannot be accessed by underage readers.

Please feel free to send me an email. Just know that these emails are filtered by my publisher. Good news is always welcome.

Jack Ryder – **jack_ryder@awesomeauthors.org**

## About the Publisher

**4Fun Publishing,** a member of **BLVNP Incorporated**, 340 S. Lemon #6200, Walnut CA 91789, info@blvnp.com / legal@blvnp.com
NOTE: Due to the highly emotional reaction of some people to works of erotic fiction, any email sent to the above address that contains foul language or religious references is automatically deleted by our anti-spam software and will not be seen. All other communications are welcome.

## DISCLAIMER

Please don't be stupid and kill yourself. This book is a work of FICTION. Do not try any new sexual practice that you find in this book. It is fiction and not to be confused with reality. Neither the author nor the publisher or its associates assume any responsibility for any loss, injury, death or legal consequences resulting from acting on the contents in this book. Every character in this book is over 18 years of age. The author's opinions are not to be construed as the opinions of the publisher. The material in this book is for entertainment purposes ONLY. Enjoy.

# Stella for Christmas
### Office Fantasy & Desires
### Romance Erotica

By: Jack Ryder

©Jack Ryder 2014
ISBN: 978-1-62761-778-9

# Chapter One

I don't really remember how Stella and I first hooked up. Literally, I don't remember it except it little fragmented snippets and erotic sexual visions that sometimes flash across my memory. It happened during the company Christmas party last year and seemed to take on a life of its own very quickly after that. And it had a very torrid and tawdry life I might add, one that led me farther down the path of depravity than I ever thought possible. Especially with the Stella I knew from work. Stella is the very best I.T. Administrator that I had ever met. She is so savvy in her duties that she is the one everyone turns to with any computer problem that arises throughout the 14 story facility that is our travel agency. I am the Vice President of Research and Acquisitions with my office on the top northwest corner of the building.

I remember the first time I saw Stella as if it were yesterday. I nearly fell out of my high back oversized leather office chair. At 6 foot 1 she is the tallest woman I had ever met. Her slender body seemed perfect in every way. Her Skirt was at a decent length but it was tight enough to show off her lovely round ass. Her shapely muscular legs seemed to go on forever and the sheer silk stockings with the seams up the back practically gave me a woody as I gawked at her.

Stella had that librarian look about her with her hair up in a bun, her white blouse buttoned up with just enough open to allow a teasing view of her upper chest. Her blazer jackets always matched her skirt color perfectly. She was always "all business" and proper etiquette in all her dealings. She called me Pete that very first day. She is the only one I have ever allowed to call me that. I have always insisted that people address me by my proper name of Peter. I did not correct her that day. It made me feel young again when she called me that. A wishful thinking.

Now, I have to stop right there and tell you that, not once did I ever even pretend to think that an old fart married man like me would ever stand a chance with a gorgeous woman like Stella. Even though she dressed rather conservatively, it was obvious to anyone who met her that she is a knockout beauty. I very quickly began to look forward to her daily visit to my office. Just so I could have a few moments alone with her and gawk at her gorgeous young body.

Almost from the start, she came up to my office every day at lunch time. Or, should I say, during the hour that Marg my secretary was gone for her lunch. I wanted to feel flattered by that, but I knew right from the start that it was because she needed a safe place to stay away from all the young hungry executives that were hounding her for a date. However, it still felt wonderful that it was ME that she wanted to feel safe with.

At 27 years old, Stella is exactly twenty years younger than me. Although my wife Nancy is a very attractive and voluptuous woman, there is just no way I could keep my eyes off of Stella. There was no way I could keep my mind from undressing her and fantasizing about all the lurid and nasty things I would love to do with her. But, again, I never in a million years would ever have thought that I could stand a chance with Stella. However, I watched my clock every day waiting for it to be 1 p.m., waiting to see her glide gracefully into my office.

As I look back, there were subtle little hints along the way. An extra button or two unfastened. Her long shapely legs draped over the arm of her plush easy chair. Little sexual innuendos in our daily banter with each other. I did feel that she truly liked me. I felt like a very privileged buddy. I always just savored every moment that I got to spend alone with her. It pleased me to no end that she seemed to enjoy my company as well.

It had been almost six months as Christmas drew near. I had learned that Stella has a deep distrust of men because she had grown up with a single mother that had dated more men than she could count. Each one had used her mother and then broke her heart when they dumped her.

She said that she preferred to take care of her own needs rather than relying on any man. I wasn't sure what that meant, but my mind raced with visions of her banging her pussy savagely with a large cock shaped dildo. She had confided she sometimes prefers the company of women when she feels lonely. You can probably guess where my mind went with that one. She also once told me that she had always wanted to take a train ride from here in Seattle all the way to Miami. That would be the longest possible route. She said it would give her plenty of time to pursue her hobby. But she never did say what that was.

Just before the Holiday, I pried out of her that her measurements are 28B-18-28. As I said earlier...she is very slender. I might add I that think that she has the most perfect body that I have ever seen. She blushed when I told her that. But I could see in her eyes that it pleased her. When she got up to leave that day, her legs swung apart a little further than normally. For a very brief moment, I saw her smooth bare slit. She was not wearing panties. I also noticed that she had a small little grin on her face when I glanced back up.

I had not planned on going to the company Christmas Party. I never go to those. I usually attend a boring family thing in the Hamptons with Nancy's family. This year I had sort of a tiff with Nancy when I disclosed that it bored me to be around her rich snobby family. She had shut me out of the bedroom that night and informed me in the morning she would take the kids to the Hamptons alone this year. She assured me that the kids love visiting her family. I had to bite my tongue on that one. The kids love the excesses that are lavished on them but are just as bored as I am. But I was NOT going to be the one to point that out to her.

**THE BUILDING** was fairly vacant that day as it normally is on Christmas Eve day. I had sent Marg home at 10 a.m. as I always do so she has plenty of time to get ready for her family gathering. I would normally be gone by now, but since Nancy had already left with the kids, there was no reason to be in a hurry. Especially since they would be gone till after the New Years. This would be the first ten days I would have alone in over 18 years. I had my feet up on the desk with a tumbler of

Brandy in my hand when Stella stepped in. "You look lonely Pete!" she said it in a teasing tone. It still thrills me when she calls me Pete.

"I need a date for the party Pete...think Nancy would lend you out for a night?" She had a silly grin on her face. She knew full well Nancy was gone. She was fully aware that there had been words before she left, that there was a wall growing between us. I noticed that Stella was not wearing her blazer today. The way her perky nipples were pressed into her blouse, it was clear that she was not wearing a bra. I felt a wiggle between my legs as I gawked at her pointy erectness. "I don't know...if that would be...wise." I was surprised how hoarse my voice sounded as I answered her.

"Come on Pete...I won't bite...too deep," she giggled it as she swung herself into the oversized chair. This time she pulled her legs up into the chair sideways. Although her skirt was still covering her front, I could very clearly see her entire ass against the soft dark leather seat. My dick was fully erect within seconds. The soft flesh of her pure white ass made me want to feel it in my hands, feel my cock engulfed in it to the hilt. "Ok, Stella...I'll be your date." I was shocked that I had said it. The word date struck guilt deep in my heart. "I'll...be your escort!" I corrected myself.

"Oooh Pete...Yes!" she shrieked it gleefully. As she jumped up out of her chair, I saw her entire ass and this time her entire bare pussy as her skirt lifted up for a moment. "Oh God," I groaned softly to myself. "This will be the best date ever...I promise!" she gasped excitedly. "It will be a night you'll never forget!" She was so exuberant that she was in my lap before I could even move. She had her arms around my neck and was kissing my neck gently. This was excruciating and exhilarating at the same point in time. The sensation of her bare ass sitting in my lap...her pussy just an inch away from the head of my throbbing prick had my mind frozen with the desire to unzip my pants and shove it into her. The thought of Nancy yelling at me before she left did little relieve this desperate lust. I was thrilled beyond words and scared to death all at the same moment. I could feel a slow ooze of fluid draining into my shorts.

When Stella let go and hopped up from my lap, I noticed that her face flushed a little as she glanced down into my lap. I was certain that she could see the huge boner bulging through my gray dress slacks. "I'm sorry, Pete...I just...got a little carried away!" I noticed that she seemed to have a little grin when she glanced back up. "I think we'll have the time of our lives!" She winked as she said it. As she bounced happily out of my office, her skirt bounced up and down too. It was several more flashes of her smooth bare ass. When I glanced down into my lap, I saw the huge wet spot on the front of my jeans. I thought that maybe I had ejaculated in my shorts without realizing it. Then I began to smell her scent. The heavy musky smell of her sex. Her bare pussy had gotten so wet that she had saturated the front of my slacks. I became so aroused and intoxicated that I rushed to my private bathroom and masturbated. My mind visualized every inch of her sexy bare ass and the wonderfully pink gash I had seen. I felt like a stupid horny teenager after I shot off. But I also cherished every instant she had been in my lap...sitting on my boner.

I left my office soon after myself pleasure. I stopped for a haircut on the way home and spent 15 minutes in the tanning booth. Things I usually do when I'm wanting to look sexy for my wife. But Nancy was far from my mind now. My mind was racing with the possibility of what might really happen. Stella had obviously gotten just as aroused as I had. She seemed to have enjoyed it. She seemed to have wanted to instigate it. The giddiness felt marvelous. I should have felt guilty when I saw Stella's stain on slacks as I removed them and the cum stain in my shorts as I pulled them off for my shower. But I felt an excited anticipation of what I hoped might be possible after all this time that I had denied myself that hope. Even though I got fully erect thinking about her in the shower, I refused to touch myself. I wanted to be completely at peak performance for her...Just in case!

# Chapter Two

"Oooh Stella… look at you!" I gasped when she opened the door to her condo. She was wearing a very short red velvet strapless dress that had a small white feathery velvet around the top edge of the dress and another all the way around the bottom hem. It fit her very snuggly and wonderfully displayed every contour of her slim sexy body. She was wearing one of those musky scents of perfume. "You look so gorgeous, Stella...Geeez, your beautiful!" I was surprised that this was the very first time I had actually told her how beautiful she is. It felt good to tell her exactly what I've felt from the very first time I saw her.

Stella bent forward and kissed me gently on the cheek. "You clean up pretty nice yourself," she chuckled softly. I wasn't sure if she was saying I looked nice in my fitted black tux or if she was referring to the mess she had made in my lap. "I'll take that as a compliment!" I whispered as I returned a kiss on her cheek. I had Robert, my chauffeur, take us to the garage entrance of the facility. Stella and I had decided to make separate entrances into the party to avoid any rumors with the work associates. Just before the elevator opened to take her up to the 12th floor, she moved forward and gave me a very quick but passionate kiss. "Just for tonight…be mine." she whispered it.

As I very slowly walked up the staircase to the 12th floor, my mind was filled with that intense kiss. I was ecstatic that she wanted me to be hers. Even if it was just for this one night. I had a momentary thought of Nancy but decided I deserved this happiness. It has been so long since.. I have felt this alive, felt this desired, felt this enamored by anything or anyone. YES...I would be Stella's tonight. I would be anything she asked of me.

I arrived at the 12th floor conference room about 10 minutes after Stella had arrived. There was already a crowd of men circled around her as I made my entrance. I saw her eyes sparkle as she saw me walk in. We took a few minutes before we finally drifted together. "I thought those guys were going to drown me with their drool," she whispered in my ear. "I thought I was going to be drunk with envy if they took another second," I whispered back. She smiled and then slightly squeezed my hand gently as we walked out to the dance floor.

She felt wonderful as she slipped into my arms. "Have I told you that you are the most handsome man I've ever met?" Her lips were so close to my ear I could feel the heat of her breath as I pulled her closer. "You're just saying that because I'm the Vice President of the company," I teased her. She pulled her head back to look directly in my eyes.

"I'm saying that because it's true!" she protested. "I'm saying it because I spent every lunch hour with you for six months. I'm saying it because I spend ten extra minutes every morning making sure my hair is perfect for you. I'm saying it because I put on an extra spritz of perfume every day and because you are the last thing I think of before sleep every night." She moved her face back next to my ear. "I'm saying it because right now my panties are wet just from you holding me." I felt her lips gently kiss my neck. "Oh God" I gasped softly.

We took a few minutes to go mingle after that dance. But my mind was frozen in time to the words she had said. All the clues had been there and yet I had never thought for a second that she could desire me like this. My eyes kept glancing over to her as other men tried their best to get her attention. It melted my heart when I saw her glancing back. One of the young men was just handing her a drink when I went to ask her to dance again. I sat both of our drinks on a table by the wall and we went to dance. "When this dance is over...take me somewhere private." Her lips were right against my ear again. "I need to kiss you...I need to feel your hands all over me," she nibbled on my earlobe before she moved her lips away from my ear.

I wasn't really sure which drink was which when I picked them up from the table. I just grabbed them and then we snuck down the hallway and up the back stairway towards my office on the 14th floor. I am not usually much of a drinker. I don't like how alcohol lowers my control of reality. But I was thirsty and swallowed nearly half of my drink in two gulps. The warmth of the alcohol going down felt good. But not nearly as good as Stella holding my hand.

As soon as we were in my office, Stella threw herself into my arms. "God…I want you, Pete,' she sort of moaned it into my mouth as she began to kiss me passionately. I ran my hands up and down her trembling back as we kissed each other like a couple of horny teenagers. When I let my hands wander up under the back of her dress, I was delighted to find her ass was bare as I squeezed on her lovely tush. "Yes…Peter…yes," she purred.

I suddenly felt weak in the knees from the lust that I was feeling. I could feel the alcohol making me feel wonderfully connected with her. "Let's use the couch," I whispered in her ear. I remember us touching each other and tearing at each other clothes. I remember her telling me that she had wanted to fuck me since the day we met. I remember that she had the most beautiful naked body I had ever seen. I remember the exquisite pleasure I felt as her hot wet pussy engulfed my prick as she lowered herself onto me.

I remember James and Stella holding me up and helping me into the elevator. I had evidently passed out after fucking Stella in my office. I remember Stella saying something to James about maybe I had been drugged as we took the elevator to the basement. I remember her giving James directions to her seaside condo down in Market Square. "Was it…OK?" I asked her in a very groggy voice in the back of my limo. "Oooh Peter…it was…wonderful, luv." I remember her kissing my neck.

I vaguely remember sliding my hand up her dress in the back of the limo and the white gooey cum that coated my fingers after I fingered her pussy. I remember being in an unfamiliar bed completely naked and watching Stella disrobe and climb into the bed next to me. But all of this is still very sketchy for me. We found out later that the drink I had consumed had contained Rohypnol…the date rage drug. We suspect that it had been meant for Stella.

I awoke at about twenty minutes before noon on Christmas day. The bed was still unfamiliar to me but the sound of my cell phone ringing on the nightstand was definitely mine. It was the special ring tone that I assigned to my wife Nancy. It is the old Elton John song "The Bitch is Back." That's a long story! When I answered the phone, Nancy was very cordial. She asked about the party, she wished me a Merry Christmas then she informed me that she wanted a separation when she returns after the first of the year.

I was just hanging up the phone as Stella walked into the bedroom carrying two cups of coffee. The momentary shock I had just felt was quickly replaced by an incredulous sense of joy. "Last night...really did...happen!" I whispered as I gawked at her beautifully exposed body. Stella was wearing one of those white chiffon transparent robe, sort of tops that has no buttons or belts. It is completely open in front, just held on with a string tied in a bow just below her neck. She is completely nude otherwise. "My God you're beautiful!" It was a soft gasp as she reached out to hand me the coffee she had brought for me.

As I took a sip of the coffee and stared at her fully erect nipples, I had a momentary memory of her telling me in the back of the limo that she has been in love with me since the very first week that she came to work. "Was that Nancy?" she asked softly as I sat my coffee on the end table next to the bed. "Yes...I think she will be filing for a divorce...soon." I replied. Although she had a look of concern in her eyes, I also noticed a hopeful sort of look on her face. "Does that mean...you will be..." I reached up and placed a finger to her lips.

I took the coffee cup out of her hand and placed it next to mine on the table. I pulled her into my arms and kissed her very greedily. "It means we can be together as much as we want!" I told her after I ended the kiss. "It means...we won't have to hide this for very long!" Before I could say anything else, she was kissing me so passionately that I thought she was going to suck all the air out of my lungs. "YOU DO WANT THIS!" It was a joyful shriek as she pulled back and cupped my face in her hands. "I thought it was just the drugs talking last night!' she panted. "I thought it would be...just a one night thing for you." Her voice had fallen to a mere whisper. As she bent forward and kissed my forehead, her perky little upturned breasts were right in my face. "I want this to be...so much more." Her confession was soft and her voice trembled.

"Oooh Peter...Oh God Yes," she moaned as I leaned forward and began to suck back and forth on both of her perky tits. The sensation of her rubbery nipples in my mouth had me hard as a rock within seconds. "Yes Peter...Yes...I'm all yours baby...I'm all yours," I felt her hand grasping my cock as she moaned it. "Oooh Yesssss Stella...Yes!" I groaned as I felt the saucey heat of her pussy sliding down my throbbing pole.

"I've wanted this forever, Peter," she purred as she impaled herself on my dong. I placed both hands on her gorgeous ass and began shoving her back and forth on my prick. "Me Too, Baby... everyday....every day," I groaned my reply. At that exact moment, I was in heaven. The fantasy that I had believed could never happen...was happening. My beautiful fantasy girl Stella was naked, riding my cock and confessing her hidden desire for me. It was not the drugs and it was not a dream or a sketchy memory. We were fucking in her bed…right here...right now." "I have wanted you so bad, baby!" The words were mumbled by her tit in my mouth.

I rocked her back and forth on my dick for a good long while as each of us professed our secret desire for one another. The sensation of her warm flesh against mine and her hot oozing fluids was the most thrilling thing I had ever experienced. I had never felt this connected and this bonded in my entire life. Not even when I lost my virginity in the back of my car as a teen, or the first night that I slept with Nancy, could compare to the heat and the passion I was feeling right now with this gorgeous woman I have wanted so desperately for so long.

It had been at least twenty minutes and I had been memorizing every moment, every emotion and every sensation. I needed to take her now...I needed to make her mine. I rolled her onto her back and shoved my dick as far into her cunt as it would go. "Oh God Yes..God Yes," she moaned. Smack, smack, smack, smack...my belly slapped against hers as I slammed myself into her faster and faster. "Take me Peter...Take all of me...Take all of me," she gasped each word as I pounded into her hungrily.

"FUCK...ME...FUCK...ME...FUCK...ME," her words were just grunts as I hammered her pussy savagely. "Oooh Stella...Here it is...Here it is baby...here it is!" My entire body vibrated as my load of semen began to flow into her vagina. I ejaculated four heavy wads of sperm deep into her hot quivering canal. "OOOH PETER... YES... YESSSSS... YES!" Her body jerked and writhed beneath me as her climax overwhelmed her.

# Chapter Three

I had called Robert my chauffeur late on Christmas day to tell him to take some time off till after the first of the year. After making sure I was OK after the drugging incident, he agreed to call me New Year's day to see what the next plan would be. "I think she is in Love with you Peter," he informed me out of the blue. "I saw the way she looked at you while we were holding you up in the elevator," he said it softly. "She is completely Goofed on you!" he added.

"ROBERT SAYS YOU'RE IN LOVE WITH ME!" I yelled it from the living room back to the bedroom where she was getting dressed as I hung up the phone. "THAT'S RIGHT, I AM!" She yelled back without hesitation. I smiled broadly. "HE SAYS YOU ARE TOTALLY GOOFED ON ME!" I yelled back. "HE'S VERY OBSERVANT! She replied. "HE SAYS YOU WANTED TO FUCK MY BRAINS OUT FOR THE REST OF MY LIFE!" I teased her. "That's right...that's my plan!" Her voice was now only a couple of feet away right here in the same room.

"Merry Christmas, Pete. That's my present. I want to be your fuck doll always!" When I glanced up, she was wearing a see thru white mesh body stocking that fit her body like a glove. It was crotchless with a large enough opening to expose her sex from above her gash all the way back to her anus. I stood up and let my bathrobe fall to the floor. I fucked her right there on her living room floor. Twice! Once in the pussy with her on her back and a second time, cup her ass with her on her knees.

ON A whim, I asked Stella if she'd like to run up the coast to Vancouver. Since we both have the augmented drivers licenses that allow you to cross back and forth into Canada, that would not be a problem. When I found that I could get a reservation on Christmas day, I booked us a room and we were soon on our way North to Canada. It as the very first time I had driven Stella's Escalade.

I was impressed with how it handled and I especially liked the very dark tinted windows that created just as much privacy as the blacked out windows in my limo. Stella had put on a chiffon top that I could see thru and a wraparound skirt which she left hanging open so I could look at her bare pussy as much as I cared to. "This is so fun," she giggled when she saw me glance down at her sex frequently. "You are so fucking sexy!" I answered her. My dick was pounding hard in my jeans.

I had pulled off the freeway in Everett to fill up with gas and Stella kept flashing her bare beaver at me through the windshield as I cleaned the glass. I loved looking at her! Last night had been the very first time I had ever seen her with her hair down. Her long silky golden blond hair in a single ponytail down to her waist. She looked so sexy sitting there in the passengers' seat smiling at me with her skirt open and her legs spread wide apart.

As I was paying for the fuel, I remembered an Adult Arcade that is just a mile up the road from this station. I had a huge grin on my face as I got back into the Escalade. "What are you up to mister?" she giggled as I started the SUV. "A night you'll never forget!" I grinned at her. I was pulling into the parking lot just a few minutes later. "Are you up for sex in public?" I asked softly. I could see her eyes glued to the car against the back fence only a few feet away. She could see the head bobbing up and down as the driver was getting sucked off. "Oooh Hell Yes," she answered softly.

I felt like the luckiest man on Earth as we walked in cuddled together with her arm wrapped around mine. I saw the clerk staring at Stella's tits through her transparent top as I paid for my admission to the Adult Theater in the back. "Ladies always free!" the clerk advised Stella. He did not bother to hide the fact he was gawking at her breasts. My dick was hard as a rock knowing he'd give anything to touch those tits. Knowing he'd love to suck on them and shove his dick in her pussy.

"Ready, Dear?" I asked softly. It took several seconds to get acclimated to the dim light as we made our way up the center aisle in the dark porn theater. As things came into focus for us, we could see several men in the very back row sucking each other off. Most of the men that we were passing had their pants down and were slowly stroking themselves. They all stared at us hungrily as we made our way to some seats. It was the fourth row from the back wall. I choose the seats two seats in from the center.

"Are you sure you are OK with this?" I whispered softly as we sat down. "Peter, I am thrilled with this!" She was already unbuttoning her blouse as she answered me. I had purposely left two seats open so some other men could come sit right next to her. I unfastened my jeans and pushed them down to my feet as Stella unwrapped the front of her skirt. She was practically nude as two men quietly moved in a filled the seats next to her. Her blouse was wide open exposing her entire front and she was naked from the waist down, sitting on her skirt.

"She is so lovely!" the man right next to her whispered over to me as I slid my hand up to her bare pussy. Her hand was already in my lap stroking my rigid prick. Both of the men next to her had their pants down to their knees and were jerking themselves as they watched me fingering her gash while she stroked me. Out of the corner of my eye, I saw the man slowly reach over and begin to fondle her tits. My dick was harder than I could ever remember.

When I pulled my fingers out of her dripping sex, I lifted them to her mouth and she sucked on them like she was giving head. "Can I suck some cocks?" she whispered in my ear very softly. "Oh yes, baby. I hoped you would want that!" I kissed her cheek. "I love you that you asked that!" I added softly as she turned around towards the man next to her. As she got on her knees in her seat facing the man, I pulled her blouse off so she was now naked except for her sandals. "Oh God Yes, Baby!" The man moaned loudly as she engulfed his pecker with her mouth.

**THERE WERE** now a half dozen other men in the row behind us all standing up and jerking their cocks as they watched Stella. I moved down behind her and slowly started to lick her crack from her pussy up to her ass pucker and back down. I could feel Stella quivering from her arousal as I ate her out while she gave head.

As soon as the man grunted and filled her mouth with spunk, the man next to him scooted in and took the first guys place. Just as she took the second dick into her mouth, one of the fellas standing behind us moaned loudly and I suddenly felt his hot semen spraying all over my face and on Stella's ass. It was the nastiest and most erotic sensation I had ever experienced.

As soon as the second fella shot his cum down Stella's throat, she turned around so she was facing the men behind us. I stood up and slipped my dick up into her drenched pussy as she began to suck off the guy directly behind us. It thrilled me to see his cock humping in and out of her mouth as I slowly see-sawed my prick in and out of her quivering cunt. There are no words to even describe the look on the faces of all the men gathered around. Each of them in utter amazement that this gorgeous young woman was eagerly servicing one and all. It seemed like my sex doll was ravenous and insatiable. As she was sucking a cock, if one of the men began to ejaculate from jerking, she would quickly move her face over to catch the cum in her mouth. By the time I jerked and filled her cunt with my semen, she had serviced 28 other men. Half of them had cum in her mouth. The other half sprayed their gooey seed all over her naked body.

Stella was a sloppy gooey mess as we made our way back out to the Escalade. The clerk nearly creamed himself when he saw all the cum matted in her hair and smeared all over her face and chest. "WE HAD A BALL!" Stella called to him as we went out the door. I saw his eyes were looking at her legs. When I glanced down, I could see my cum running down the inside of her legs. I lifted up the back of her skirt to expose her bare ass to him. "Oh My God," he groaned softly.

Right there next to the car at the back of the parking lot, Stella stripped naked again. She used the blouse to wipe all the cum off her face and body and then she smoothed it out of her hair as best she could. After she slowly put her hair back into a ponytail, she opened the back of the vehicle and bent over to get a dress out of her travel bag in the back. "Oh, my God! That's beautiful!" The voice came from the car parked next to us. The man inside was staring at her bare ass bent over the back of the car. "You lucky bastard!" he groaned. I saw him shudder as he shot his load down the throat of the girl that was sucking his cock. "Thank you!" Stella told him brazenly as she pulled her very indecently short tube dress on to cover herself.

The border crossing into Canada wasn't quite as painless as we had expected. It wasn't a big deal really. More of a funny inconvenience. We were directed to the inspection area rather than just being waved through. It became immediately obvious that the gate guard wanted a closer look at Stella. As he looked at her license and then down at her lap for the 10th time, she very coyly spread her legs and sat back so he could clearly see her pussy.

"Is there something else you'll need to see officer?" She spread her legs even farther apart. His hand trembled as he handed her license back. "That...that...will be...all," he stuttered. It was clear to see that he had a huge bulge in his trousers as he finally waved us through. Stella was so excited by his arousal that she sucked me off on the way to the hotel. "I think...we will be so marvelous together," she said it as she was wiping her mouth with the back of her hand after I shot off in her mouth. "Meeee too baby...Meeee too!" I chuckled.

Stella and I spent the next five days sightseeing around Vancouver. It was pretty cold since it was now winter. But that did not deter Stella from finding ways for us to have an audience for our sexual adventures. She fucked me at the loading platform at the train station. It was during the evening rush hour and we just managed to have a quickie before we had to make a dash for the stairwell when we saw a policeman trying to make his way to us.

Stella gave me a hand job in a darkened restaurant on the second evening. We were seated in the back corner and Stella lifted her skirt up for the three young men that were facing our table. Once she had their attention, she opened my slacks and jerked me off while they watched. I got so aroused watching them as she stroked me that I blew a huge load all over her arm. She then used my spunk as a lubricant to masturbate herself while the three men watched. I think this was the exact moment that I decided that I wanted this gorgeous woman forever.

On New Year's Eve day, we woke up to a beautiful clear sunny day. As Stella threw open the drapes to let in the sunny day, she noticed two men out on the balcony in the high-rise across the street. It was immediately obvious to her that they had seen her standing there naked. "Come here and fuck me, Pete." She whispered it. "I have a fan club watching," she giggled softly. As I approached her from behind, I could see them standing by the front rail. One of them had just come back onto the balcony with a pair of binoculars.

I slipped in behind her and acted as if no one was there. "Yesssss Baby," she purred as I slid my hands up to her tits and fondled her as I kissed her neck from behind. I felt her press back against me as I pulled on her nipples gently. As I saw the men swapping the binoculars back and forth, I slid my right hand down her belly to Stella's dripping pussy and began to bang my fingers in and out as they watched. Just as they pulled their pants down and started to jerk off, I saw a third young man appear. As he raised his very large professional video camera to focus in on us, it seemed like he was familiar to me.

"Fuck me. Put your big dick in my cunt and fuck me!" Stella's voice was husky and full of lust. I bent my knees and slipped my cock up into her gash from behind and buried myself in her to the hilt. "Take me, Peter...Take me!" She gasped. Smack, smack, smack, smack... I had both hands on her hips and I pounded her ruthlessly as the man across the way recorded every moment of it.

Stella stared directly at the camera so the passion and pleasure was recorded as I filled her with my semen. "Thank you, love....I wanted to end the year right!" she giggled as I pulled my dick out of her cum drenched pussy.

It had thrilled me to watch those men jerking off and the other man recording us. I was deeply in love as she stood there with my cum oozing out.

# Chapter Four

I got a call from Robert that last day of the year. I had instructed him to hire a private investigator to look into the drugging incident on Christmas Eve. Robert called that morning to report the progress of that investigation.

They found that the drink had been given to Stella by a young man who was a fictitious "New Employee" named Brad. My mind suddenly recognised him as the same young man I had just seen with the video camera. They had learned that Brad is really the personal assistant for my wife Nancy. He worked directly for her father...the Senator.

"Get any yummy photos?" I quipped hopefully. "Better than that!" Robert blurted out. "He got us some videos!" He then informed me that he got a video of Nancy sucking Brad off in the back of her Mercedes limo. He had a video of them fucking in the boat house behind her father's mansion. And a third video of Nancy bent over her father's desk being fucked up the ass by her happy assistant. "Don't ask how he got the videos!" Robert sort of whispered it. "You really don't want to know!"

I must confide that I was very happy by the time we got off the phone. Now I would have at least an equal bargaining chip when Nancy and I get divorced. Not that I want to cause her any problems. I just want to protect my...interests. Just after lunch, I called Nancy. I was very cordial. I informed her that I would be moving into our Downtown Condo for the separation. I also told her that I would expect to keep that property when the separation becomes a divorce.

When Nancy tried to say it was too early to speak of divorce, I cut her off. "Say hello to Brad for me...and thank him for the best night I'll never remember!" I taunted her. When she fell silent, I added, "And for the personal services he provides for you...so vigorously!" I hung up before she could say another word.


STELLA AND I arrived at the Gentlemen's Club at just after 9 p.m. that New Year's Eve. We had been invited by the owner, a former client who had sold his travel agency to our company and used the money to purchase this club. We have remained friends ever since. I always enjoy complete access to the club any time I am in the area.

Since it is a private club, tonight's party would be a no-holds-barred swinger's gang bang. I knew that Stella would delight in the sex fest we were about to participate in. She was already giddy with excitement as we pulled into the parking lot. I saw Brad pulling into the lot just a few moments later. I secretly instructed the bouncer at the door to let him in even though he was not on the guest list. Stella and I had a plan for our nosey tail.

Brad was in and seated on the opposite side of the room within a couple of minutes. He had just ordered his first drink when we sent Molly over to him. Molly is a knockout little redhead exotic dancer at the club. We have hired her to seduce our snooping buddy Brad. Her creamy white skin and voluptuous body will be difficult for him to resist. Her skimpy bikini top is so tiny that it barely covers her nipples. Her huge round tits are practically in his face as she bent over to ask if he would like some company.

Brad took the bait within just a few moments. We could see his eyes riveted to her breasts as Molly sat next to him and whispered. We saw the lust on his face when she reached into his lap to rub on his rapidly swelling prick. Brad was all smiles when Molly took his hand and led him to one of the lap dance booths along the back wall. I took some photos of that with the digital camera I had brought with me.

I got more photos of Molly grinding on his lap. I snapped several more when he yanked her top off and started to suck greedily on her huge jugs. I took two of Molly French kissing him and then holding hands while she led him upstairs to the private bedroom. The rest would be video recorded by the secret hidden camera inside the bedroom.

Now we were ready in earnest. Molly would keep Brad occupied until after midnight when Stella and I would be ready to finish with him. But we were here for fun too. Stella looked so magnificent in her nearly transparent white jersey style dress that fit her like a glove. We had seen several couples eyeing us throughout the evening. This is a swinger's party after all! We got up to go mingle the moment that Molly took Brad upstairs.

Gloria and Phillip were the first couple that we approached. "Would you like to see a little more of me?" Stella asked him straight out. We had noticed that Phillip walked past us about a half dozen times over the last hour. He had not hidden the fact that he was looking at Stella's perky tits since he could clearly see them through the thin fabric. Stella pulled the top of her dress down till her breasts were fully exposed to him. "Go ahead...play with them all you want," she invited as she sat down on his lap. "Oooh Geeeezus, you're gorgeous!" His voice quivered as he began to gently fondle her tits.

"Is there anything you would like?" I asked Gloria softly as I sat down next to her. I placed my hand on her bare thigh and slowly moved it up into her miniskirt till I was just touching her dripping gash. She was already drenched as I shoved two fingers up into her cunt. "Oooh Yes... do thaaaaaaaat!" she moaned. I pulled her top down to expose her huge 38D tits. They were swaying slightly as her body twitched while I finger fucked her.

Gloria was delighted when I got on my knees between her legs and pushed her skirt up to her waist. "Oooh, Phillip...look at this," she moaned loudly as I began to slurp on her dripping hole. But Phillip was already vibrating and too lost in his own pleasure with Stella on her knees sucking him off. His head was thrashing back and forth as hers bobbed up and down on his prick.

It aroused me tremendously as I glanced around the club. There were couples everywhere engaged in fellatio or just fucking openly for all to admire. I also noticed that Bob and Lilly at the next table were still alone even though several couples had approached them. Their eyes were riveted to me and Stella as they gently fondled each other while they watched us. They would be next!

I could feel Gloria quivering as she neared her orgasm. Phillip suddenly began to grunt and moan as he emptied his seed into Stella's mouth. Out of the corner of my eye I could see him jerking and twitching as she sucked on his spitting knob like a hoover. "Oooh Geeeezus...Yes... Yes...Yesssss!" Gloria's body started to convulse as I got her off. They were both still panting for air when Stella and I stepped over to the next table.

I have had my eye on Lilly since we first came into the club. She is different than my gal in every way. At 5 foot 1 she is a foot shorter than Stella. She is so petite that she is probably a size one. Her coal black hair is in a very short style similar to Anne Hathaway. Her perky little tits are very small but she has huge puffy pink nipples that I can see through her transparent top. I am looking forward to bouncing her up and down on my prick.

Stella had also taken a fancy to Bob. She had told me earlier that she loved how he looked at her like a little lost puppy each time she saw him glancing at her. She had told me; "I can't wait to rock his world!" She was smiling at him coyly as we approached them. Her dress still pulled down exposing her breasts. "Is this seat taken?" she said it softly as she straddled his legs and sat down facing him. Her breasts were just inches from her face. "It's....reserved...for you!" he gasped lustfully.

"I guess that leaves me and you! I winked at Lilly as I teased her. Lilly reached directly forward and began to unfasten my dress slacks. "I guess we'll just have to make do!" Her smart ass reply thrilled me. "Oooh God Yes...You'll do!" I groaned as she engulfed my prick with her hot drooling mouth.

Gluck, gluck, gluck, gluck...Lilly made little gagging noises as she shoved more and more of my cock down her throat. It was fascinating to watch Bob's dick humping in and out of my Stella while his wife was sucking my dick. I stepped back for a moment to allow Lilly to strip naked for me. "Put that big delicious cock in me!" she demanded as soon as she was bare.

I placed both hands around her waist and lifted her up effortlessly. "Oooh Peter...that's soooo... good!" she moaned loudly as I sat her down on my prick till she was impaled on it. She wrapped her legs around my waist as I grabbed her ass cheeks and shoved her up and down on my rigid dick. She had her arms around my neck and her head tilted back as she totally lost herself in the pleasure of my 9 inch prick stretching her pussy over and over as I humped into her. "so good.... so good," she moaned.

"OH STELLA! OH STELLA! OH STELLA!" Bob's legs were quivering as he shot his load up into Stella's womb.

As Stella climbed off his prick, I saw a long rope of his semen drain out of her pussy as she sat down next to him. My dick was so hard it felt like it might explode at any moment. I lifted Lilly off my dick and bent her over the table right in front of Stella and plowed back into her cunt from behind.

Smack, smack, smack, smack...I savagely pounded into her. I was ecstatic when Stella bent forward and began to kiss Lilly very passionately. Watching them kiss one another was so damn erotic that I erupted into Lilly. My dick shot off four heavy wads of sperm into her drenched pussy flooding her till it began to ooze out. "Oooh Peter...Oooh Peter...Oooh Peter." The sensation of my hot seed flowing into her sent Lilly over the edge too.

It was now 15 minutes till midnight so the four of us decided to just rest so we would be ready for the big moment. I had promised Stella that I would be inside her when the New Year arrives. I was enchanted as I watched Stella and Lilly while we were chatting over the next several minutes. They continually petted and touched each other so tenderly. During the conversation we learned that they also lived in the Seattle area and were also good friends with Joe, the owner of this club. Bob confided that this was the third year they had come to Vancouver for New Years.

I was very pleased that my cock was at full erection when Stella climbed onto my lap and two minutes before. With a little coaxing by Stella and Lilly, Bob was erect just in time for Lilly to climb on with 30 seconds left. As all the horns and bells signaled that the New Year was here, I pulled Stella forward and kissed her passionately. When I released her, Lilly leaned over and started kissing Stella as they both rocked back and forth in unison. It was so HOT watching them.

As we rested after Bob and I finally shot off, we exchanged phone numbers so we can hook up together again back in Seattle. "This is going to be the best year ever!" Lilly announced softly. "When I was a child, my mother told me that whatever you are doing at midnight on New Year's will be exactly what you will do all year!" After a stunned silence, I bent forward and kissed her on the cheek. "This WILL be the best year ever!" I agreed.

# Chapter Five

Bradley was delighted with his good fortune. He had been instantly attracted to Molly the moment he walked into the club. He had watched her pole dancing as he found his seat in the back corner. Although his main concern had been to stay out of plain sight for his intended assignment, he had been pleased that he was in the perfect spot to watch this lovely creamy skinned girl humping the pole. *"Damn...I'd give anything to have some of that!"* He thought to himself. His cock was swelling as he watched her.

Brad was not happy with his present situation. He had agreed to be the Senator's daughter's personal assistant with the expectation of a much better posting soon after. He never imagined that it would include having to hump the old broad 12 years his senior. Nor did he believe that he would still be stuck with her these two years later. *"This is the sort of girl I deserve!"* He told himself. *"I could fall in love with that!"* His mind wandered as he was now fully erect.

Stella and Peter had paid Molly two grand to service this fella. *"Not hard on the eyes"* she noted to herself as she approached. "Is this seat taken?" Molly had made it a point to leave her tiny top very loose so as she bent forward, Brad could clearly see both of her coral pink nipples. After fondling him and telling him that she was free for the night, she informed him that it was literal...she was FREE! Getting him back to the secret bedroom had been a cinch once she had let his cock wanted into her gash during the lap dance out front.

Brad could not ever remember his cock being so hard as Molly removed her bikini and mounted his twitching pecker. The sensation of her sweet hot pussy engulfing his dick was exquisite. "Oooh Yeah, Baby...Fuck Me...Fuck Me!" He groaned loudly. He had both hands on her creamy white ass helping her to ride his prick as he sucked greedily on her tits. *"This must be heaven!"* He thought to himself. It all felt so wonderfully dreamy.

Brad passed out just after he shot his load up into Molly. She made it a point to perch over him for a few more moments so the camera could record his cum oozing out of her sex. Then she bent forward and whispered in his ear; "Remember me always baby!" After she got dressed, she turned off the video camera and locked him inside the room. The Rohypnol that she had put in his drink earlier would keep him out till tomorrow morning. "Sweet Dreams," she giggled as she walked up the hall.

**IT WAS** a half hour into the New Year when Stella and I stepped into the bedroom where Brad was passed out. "How's it feel asshole?" I whispered down at him as I set up my digital camera tripod. Stella straddled his face naked and squatted down just far enough to make it look like he was eating her pussy. I took several photos of that with his arms draped around her back so it appeared that he was holding her.

Then I took several photos of Stella sitting on his prick. From behind, you could not tell that his eyes were closed or that his dick was completely flaccid under her grinding pussy. The final shot was of my cum dripping out of her pussy onto his thigh right above his very recognisable heart tattoo on his leg.

After we got him dressed, which wasn't easy with him being dead weight, we took him out tohid Humvee that the bouncer had already parked in the alleyway for us. Once we had him lying in the back seat, we covered him in a couple of blankets and locked him in. We tried to tip the bouncer for helping us load him into the vehicle, but he refused us. He told it was his pleasure to help us even the score.

It was a little after 1 a.m. when we returned to the party. We found Molly sitting at the bar talking to the bartender. "There is one more thing we would like to do with you!" I whispered it in her ear as I cupped her breasts from behind and started fondle them. "We want to thank you personally!" I felt her trembling as she leaned back against me. Stella had moved in next to us and now had a hand inside Molly's bikini bottom rubbing her pussy. "That...would be...nice," Molly moaned softly.

I reached down and untied Molly's bikini. Sensing what I wanted next, she scooted back to the edge of the bar stool and I slipped my rigid prick up into her drenched gash. "Oooh, my God! Yes!" Her moan was muffled because she was now sucking on Stella's right breast. I was surprised and thrilled when the bartender moved behind Stella and began fondling her naked body. "Yes! Fuck Me!" Stella invited him. He quickly dropped his pants and shoved his prick into her.

It was tremendously erotic to watch Stella and Molly kissing and fondling and sucking on each other as we humped them from behind. This was an entirely and new and exciting part of Stella that thrilled me deeply. It was marvelous to see her filled with such passion each time she played with another woman.

I exploded into Molly's pussy and filled her with so much cum that it flowed out of her and pooled on the seat of the barstool. Within moments, the bartender began to vibrate as he emptied his seed into Stella. Before we left, we gave Molly our phone number so she can come visit any time she is in the Seattle area. They kissed one more time very passionately at the door as we left.

**THE SENATOR** was not pleased when he watched the DVD that he had received anonymously. He was disgusted as he found that his Daughter has been banging her personal assistant. This could adversely affect his upcoming election. He quickly called his secretary to get Brad in his office...NOW! Then he dialed his daughter's cell phone number.

Nancy was stunned as she turned off her DVD player. Not only had she just watched herself having sex with Brad in three separate locations, but she had also watched Brad fucking some cute little redhead and then that bitch that's banging her husband. Nancy was raging mad. Brad had betrayed her in the most damaging and most humiliating way. His lust driven actions would be devastating beyond repair.

Brad was stunned as he left the Senators office. "FIRED...how on Earth...I did exactly what he *asked!*" He fumed inside. Brad had no clue about the DVD's that had been sent. He smiled warmly as he saw Nancy approaching quickly in the long hallway. SMACK... Nancy slapped him dead in the face. "You son of a bitch!" she screamed. "You fucked up any leverage I might have had in the divorce!" SMACK... She slapped him again. "You just couldn't keep that dick in your pants!" Brads face was stinging as Nancy stormed off towards her father's office.

There was a small package waiting in the mail box when Brad got home. Inside, there was a DVD with a small envelope taped to it. There was one word on the envelope: ENJOY! Brad got a knot in his stomach as he thumbed through the photos that were in the envelope. There was some of him chatting with that cute redhead up in Vancouver. Then, there were some of her in his lap with her tits in his face and his cock buried in her pussy in the lap dance booth.

The next bunch of photos was that gorgeous blond that he has been spying on. She was sitting on his face. Then she was fucking him. Then, his cum draining out of her pussy onto his thigh right next to his tattoo. Brad could not remember any of this happening. But it was obviously him underneath her. When he watched the video of Molly fucking him in the same bed, he understood how completely screwed he was now.

**I COULD** tell that Nancy was livid when I showed up at the divorce hearing with Stella on my arm. Her eyes were ablaze as she glanced up and down. Stella had worn an indecently short black mini skirt with high heels and sheer black stockings with the seam up the back. Her white chiffon blouse barely concealed her braless tits and it was unbuttoned far enough to display a good amount of cleavage. Nancy had to bit her tongue. The Senator had demanded that she get this over with immediately.

Stella and I sold our condos in Seattle and bought a new property just across the sound on Vashon Island. It was a lovely three bedroom-home with a full acre of property facing the sound. It was the property right next to where Bob and Lilly live. It was a new place where the four of us would spend most nights together. Visited often by Molly.

As time went by, she and Robert became quite an item. As I look back, I may not ever remember that Christmas Eve. But Stella is by far, the best *Christmas Gift* I ever received!

*THE END*

Here is a sample from another story you may enjoy:

# JACK RYDER

# TRAILER TRASH
# Payback
## Sweet Revenge

# ADULT EROTIC ROMANCE

**WE SPENT** most of Saturday watching the movers as they loaded the moving van, hauled our belongings to the trailer and then unloaded the van. That evening, we spent moving all the furniture around until we were happy with where each item was. As I was unpacking a couple of boxes that contained the bed sheets and bath towels, I happened to glance out the bedroom window. I could see a young blond hair woman in the trailer across from me. She was completely naked.

She was staring right at me with a slight grin. I was frozen as she moved closer to the window. From what I could see, she looked to be about maybe 23 years old. Her yellow blond hair was in a ponytail and her small perky tits had a slight upturn that made them deliciously sexy. She gave a little wave and then the blinds came down.

There was a sudden noise behind me and I jumped. "It's just me silly!" Anna laughed as she entered the room. "And what are you thinking about?" she giggled playfully when she saw the lump in my jeans. I could see one of the slats open in the blinds across the way. I could see her fingers pulling it farther down as I stood up. I know that she could easily see the bulge even from twenty feet away. "I was thinking how nice this would feel buried in your sweet pussy!" I lied to Anna.

I reached for Anna and pulled her to the bed. "I want you now…I want to break in our new home," I told her softly as I began to pull her sweat pants down. Before she could complain about the window being wide open, I bent down and began licking up and down her smooth bare slit.

"Oh Yes..Yes...Yesss," Anna moaned as I pulled her sweat pants completely off.

"The window...the wind…ooooh…my God Yes." Anna's body shuddered as I drove my cock into her pussy in one brutal thrust. I glanced over and saw the blinds opening slightly as I began to pound into Anna's hot wet gash. I lifted myself up with my arms so my secret audience could see every inch of my prick see sawing in and out Anna. "Take Me...Take me, Dex" Anna gasped.

It thrilled me that I could see her silhouette in her blinds as she watched me banging my wife. I imagined that she was fingering herself. I could practically see her delicious little tits rising and falling as she masturbated. That thought sent me over the edge. "HERE IT IS BABY...HERE IT IS!" As I began to ejaculate, I pulled my dick out and scooted up so my cum sprayed all over Anna's tits. I could just see her eyes for a moment through the slat. Then she closed it tight.

I felt a little guilty that I had cum so quickly and had not satisfied Anna yet. "We're not done yet baby!" I panted softly. I kissed her tenderly as I smeared the semen all over her tits. "I love how sexy your tits feel with me all over them," I whispered in her ear. I continued to smear it all over while I scooted down and started to lick her pussy again. "Yes Baby...Eat Me...Eat Me," Anna moaned as she began to hump herself up into my face.

My dick was quickly swelling again as I thought about the young girl who had been watching us earlier. I could feel Anna's body thrashing beneath me as I brought her closer to her climax.

"OH YES...FUCK ME, DEX...FUCK ME!" It was that deep husky moan that I love so much. Anna was just beginning to jerk underneath me as I drove into her and fucked her savagely as she screamed my name and convulsed uncontrollably. My dick erupted, spitting three huge wads of semen deep into her womb.

We both laid there panting deeply for air for several minutes. When she finally regained her composure, Anna kissed me gently on the cheek. "That was...sensational," she whispered as I rolled off of her. "I wanted our first....to be...special!" I glanced out our window and saw the light in the other bed room finally go out. I was smiling broadly as Anna kissed me again and assured me that it was very special.

Anna and I spent most of the day Sunday unpacking boxes and putting everything away in our new little home. Although I was very pleased with all of the space we had in the three bedroom trailer, Anna complained continually about it being so much smaller than our old home. Late in the afternoon, Anna suddenly told me that she needed to go for a drive and "take a break". I was happy to have the time alone. I felt it would be a good break for the both of us.

Several minutes after she left, I heard a buzzing noise coming from near the couch in the living room. When I located the noise, I found Anna's cell phone on the end table next to the couch. I hesitated a few moments, struggling whether or not a should peek at the text message she had received. My curiosity finally got the best of me and I opened the message.

*"Waiting for you, Baby...Been horny for you all day... I'll be in bed waiting...Naked!"*

If you enjoyed this sample then look for **Trailer Trash Payback**.

**Also by this Author**

## About the Author

Jack Ryder LOVES everything there is about sex!

When he is not involved with his "swinger" friends, enjoying a steamy threesome, or being part of a raunchy "gang bang", you can find him on first class planes, trains, and cruise ships. Traveling seems to be the BEST way to finding new and interesting sexmates for him. Sexmates. Plural. He lives with the saying "The More, The Merrier!"

He owns a successful business in New York. He writes as a hobby and also as sort of documentation of his mind-blowing sexcapades over the years. He is presently roaming around the streets of Manhattan but can be anywhere in the world too, since he travels often. So, beware! You just might be his next mate.

*"The most fun thing I enjoy when writing my stories is trying to figure out which is fantasy and which was memory. ENJOY! (Preferably with a friend. \*wink\*)"-Jack Ryder-*

## From the Author

If you have any comments, suggestions, or would just like to get a little personal, please feel free to email me at:
<u>jack_ryder@awesomeauthors.org</u>

If you enjoyed any of my books then please share the love and click like on my books in Amazon.

If you write me a review and send me an email I will send you a free book, or many.
(Just know that these emails are filtered by my publisher.)

Good news is always welcome.

One Last Thing, For Kindle Readers...

When you turn the page, Kindle will give you the opportunity to rate this book and share your thoughts on Facebook and Twitter. If you enjoyed my writings, would you please take a few seconds to let your friends know about it? Because... when they enjoy they will be grateful to you and so will I.

Thank You!

**Jack Ryder**
jack_ryder@awesomeauthors.org

www.ingramcontent.com/pod-product-compliance
Lightning Source LLC
Chambersburg PA
CBHW071353130626
46556CB00005B/2169